D0104705

"HELLO READING books are a perfect introduction to reading. Brief sentences full of word repetition and full-color pictures stress visual clues to help a child take the first important steps toward reading. Mastering these storybooks will build children's reading confidence and give them the enthusiasm to stand on their own in the world of words."

—Bee Cullinan
Past President of the International Reading
Association, Professor in New York University's
Early Childhood and Elementary Education Program

"Readers aren't born, they're made. Desire is planted—planted by parents who work at it."

—Jim Trelease
author of *The Read-Aloud Handbook*

"When I was a classroom reading teacher, I recognized the importance of good stories in making children understand that reading is more than just recognizing words. I saw that children who have ready access to storybooks get excited about reading. They also make noticeably greater gains in reading comprehension. The development of the HELLO READING stories grows out of this experience."

—Harriet Ziefert
M.A.T., New York University School of Education
Author, Language Arts Module,
Scholastic Early Childhood Program

For Harriet

PUFFIN BOOKS
Published by the Penguin Group
Viking Penguin, a division of Penguin Books USA Inc.,
375 Hudson Street, New York, New York 10014, U.S.A.
Penguin Books Ltd, 27 Wrights Lane, London W8 5TZ, England
Penguin Books Australia Ltd, Ringwood, Victoria, Australia
Penguin Books Canada Ltd, 2801 John Street, Markham, Ontario, Canada L3R 1B4
Penguin Books (N.Z.) Ltd, 182-190 Wairau Road, Auckland 10, New Zealand

Penguin Books Ltd, Registered Offices: Harmondsworth, Middlesex, England

First published in Picture Puffins 1991

3 5 7 9 10 8 6 4 2

Text copyright © Fred Ehrlich, 1991
Illustrations copyright © Martha Gradisher, 1991
All rights reserved
Library of Congress catalog number: 90-53550
ISBN 0-14-054393-7

Printed in Singapore for Harriet Ziefert, Inc.

LUNCH BOXES

Fred Ehrlich
Pictures by Martha Gradisher

PUFFIN BOOKS

At Oak Hill School it's time to eat.
The teachers like it when we're neat.

See how quietly we pass
To the lunchroom from our class.

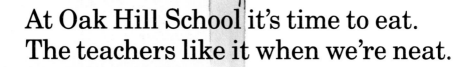

Miss Vanilla
Room 101

Ms. Vanilla and Mr. Blair
Tell each child to take a chair.

Everyone's in a happy mood
As they sit down to eat their food.

Then Antonia drops her cheese

And tries to catch it with her knees.

Paul starts mixing soggy toast
With applesauce and day-old roast.

Charlene, eat your Cheerios.
Please don't put them up your nose.

Ben, you are mushing your banana
In a most disgusting manner.

Donald's mouth opens wide
A whole cupcake fits inside.

Angelina, what's the use
Of dunking hot dogs in your juice?

Mary says that Lee Wong's dumb.
He sat on her purple plum.

Lee Wong says that Mary's fat
And has a face just like a cat.

When Rosa's milk spills on the floor
She tries to drink it with a straw.

Melba takes a hard-boiled egg
And throws it to her best friend Greg.

"Peanut butter in your hair!
Stop that now!" yells Mr. Blair.

Ms. Vanilla's turning red.
A sandwich hit her on the head.

Benita says to Mary Ann
Please be quiet if you can.

Don't you see that Mr. Blair
Has started looking like a bear?

And I think that Ms. Vanilla
Is sounding like a big gorilla.

"Clean the tables. Clean the floor."

"We can't stand this anymore."

"Finish lunch," says Mr. Blair.
"Put your garbage over there."

See how quietly we pass
Out the door and back to class.